For Charlotte, whose laughter is her special sound.

First Edition

When Rex becomes envious of other animals' special sounds,
Timmy takes Rex to the zoo on a sound-finding mission.

Bahart Publications

Eight Legs Publishing

Book design by Andrew Baron

ISBN 0-9760348-3-2

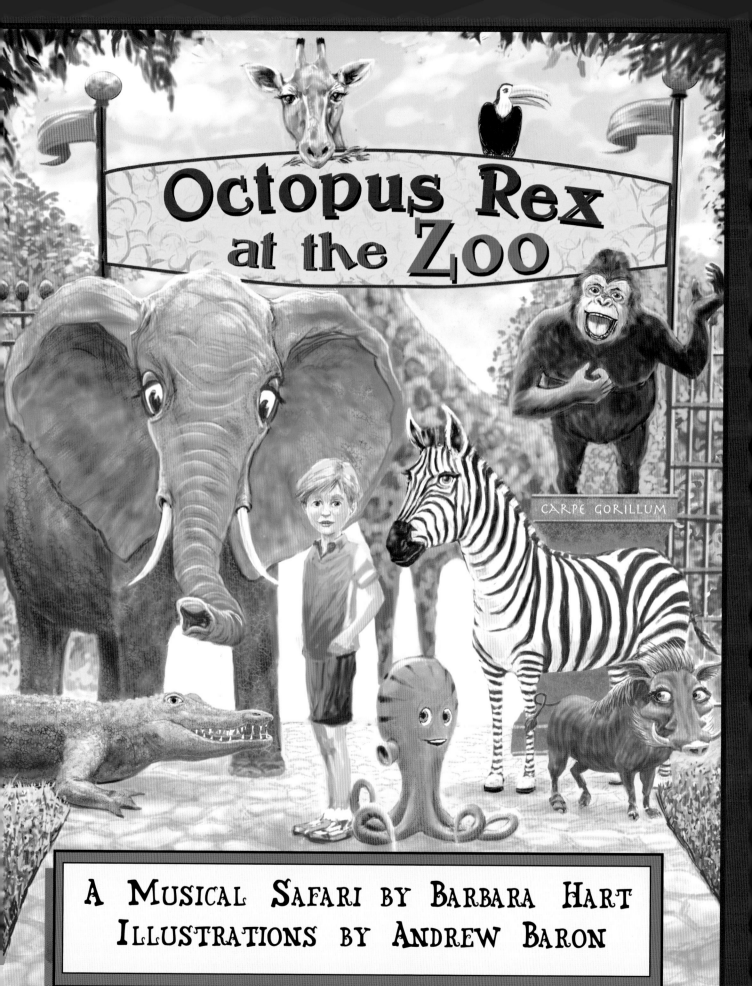

Octopus Rex at the Zoo

CARPE GORILLUM

A MUSICAL SAFARI BY BARBARA HART
ILLUSTRATIONS BY ANDREW BARON

"Hurry up and finish your breakfast," said Timmy's mom. "It's almost eight o'clock. You don't want to be late meeting Rex."

Timmy gulped down his juice. "I hope he remembers; we made a pact."

"Oh, I'm certain he'll be there," assured Timmy's mom. "And I hope you two learned your lesson last year not to keep Rex out of the water too long."

"Oh, we'll be careful, I promise," said Timmy.

"I believe you," said Timmy's mom. "Have fun, but be back by five."

"OK," shouted Timmy as he ran out the door. He couldn't believe this day was finally here.

When he got to the beach, he hurried to the blue umbrella where he and Rex had agreed to meet. He didn't see Rex anywhere on the sand.

Finally, he spotted Rex out in the ocean. He was bobbing up and down alongside some boys who were on surfboards. A big wave was coming up behind them. Timmy tried to warn Rex: "Rex, watch out for the waaaave!"

Too late. Rex didn't hear Timmy's warning. The wave came crashing down on top of Rex. He tumbled over and over in the swirling surf until he was washed up on the shore. He lay there sputtering and coughing.

Timmy ran over to Rex. "I seem to remember picking you up off the sand last year," he laughed as Rex grabbed onto his hand.

"Yeah, I remember," said Rex, while he brushed the sand off his arms and wiped the water from his eyes. He looked up at Timmy. "You look taller than you were last summer."

"I am. I've grown two inches," replied Timmy proudly. "I'm the tallest boy in my class."

"I've grown too," said Rex, standing up straight. "Can you tell?"

"Uh, which way?" asked Timmy.

"My arms are longer, I think," replied Rex. "See?" Rex stretched his arms out as far as he could.

"Yeah, sure," agreed Timmy, not wanting to hurt his friend's feelings. "Hey, Rex, aren't you going to give me five?"

"I'll give you five if you give me five," teased Rex. During the year Rex had shown all of his octopus friends how to high-five. They even had a secret high-five club under the ocean.

Timmy looked at Rex and grinned. "Yeah, Rex, I'll give you five!"

Gimme Five (CD Track 2)

(Timmy):
Gimme five my friend
You're back again
I've waited for this day
When we would be together
To run and laugh and play
We'll slide down a sand dune
Then climb back up again
That's what we'll do this summer
Gimme five again

(Rex):
Gimme five my friend, I'm back again
I've been waiting too
I've dreamed about the games we'll play
And all the things we'll do
I'll be Silver Surfer
You be Superman
That's what we'll do this summer
Gimme five again

(Both):   This time we'll be careful
           This time we'll be smart
(Rex):   Please don't let me dry up and die
(Timmy): I promise, cross my heart

(Both):
Gimme five, my friend, around the bend
We'll find a carousel
We'll ride the magic horses
And munch on caramel
We'll float down the river
Like Tom Sawyer and Huck Finn
That's what we'll do this summer
Gimme five again
That's what we'll do this summer
Gimme five again
Whistle
Gimme five again, yeah!

"Remember, we have to be very careful and make sure you get back to the water in time," cautioned Timmy as they started walking toward town.

"I know. I won't forget," promised Rex.

As they passed by Mrs. Hobson's cottage, Rex pointed to a funny looking creature sitting on the porch. It's body was long like a sausage, supported by four, very short, stubby legs. And it was making loud yippy noises. "What is that?" asked Rex.

"That's a dog," replied Timmy. "It's Mrs. Hobson's pet dachshund, Schnitzel. She likes to bark at people."

"Bark? What's a bark?" asked Rex.

"It's the sound that dogs make," replied Timmy. "Dogs bark, cats meow, ducks quack. Every animal has its own special sound."

"Do I have a special sound?" Rex wanted to know.

"Well, I'm not sure," answered Timmy, "but I don't think so. It would sound pretty silly under the water. I've never heard a fish make noise."

"My mom says whales sing to each other, and *they* live under the water," declared Rex.

"That's true, but a whale isn't a fish--it's a mammal," Timmy explained with authority. "I learned about whales last fall when my grandfather took me whale watching."

Rex looked very confused. He would have to ask his mother why whales had a special sound and he didn't.

"I've got a great idea," said Timmy. "Let's go to the zoo."

"What's the zoo?" asked Rex excitedly, ready for adventure.

"It's a place where they keep wild animals so people can go look at them and learn about them. It's really neat," said Timmy. "Harry the ape is my favorite. He's really a gorilla, which is a type of ape. He's smart, too. He knows sign language."

"Sign language?" Again, just like last summer, Rex was full of questions. There were so many things to learn.

"It's talking with your hands; it's called signing," explained Timmy. "People who can't hear or talk use sign language to communicate with each other. Harry's trainer teaches visitors how to sign so they can communicate with Harry. Come on, I'll show you."

As soon as they got to the zoo, Timmy started running to the area where the gorillas were kept. Rex ran as fast as he could to keep up with Timmy. "There he is!" shouted Timmy.

Harry was sitting with his arms crossed in front of him. His dark eyes followed Timmy and Rex as they walked up to the fence. Timmy waved at Harry and started talking to him in sign language. Harry signed back.

"What are you saying?" Rex wanted to know.

"We said hi to each other, and I told him who you are and what you are," replied Timmy.

"That looks like fun," exclaimed Rex, trying to imitate Harry and Timmy. He started wiggling his arms in front of Harry, pretending to sign. Harry, of course, didn't understand any of Rex's ridiculous motions.

"You can't do sign language with eight arms," explained Timmy. Rex didn't care. He continued waving his arms wildly in front of Harry.

"Hey Harry, sing your special song for Rex," begged Timmy as he signed to Harry.

Harry didn't need to be asked twice. He rose up on his big, hairy knuckles and cleared his throat. By this time lots of people had gathered around. Harry was famous for his ability to sing. No other ape in the zoo could do this. Rex stood there wide-eyed as Harry began to sing.

Harry Ape (CD Track

I'm a big ol' hairy ap
I'm big and hairy and stror
I was put into this zo
So you could look at me all day lor
I'm supposed to dance, I'm supposed to pranc
I'm supposed to a-mus
Your every wish is my comman
You know I can't refus

Like I know you like to see me scratc
And I like to scratch a lo
Guess today's your lucky da
I'm gonna scratch everything I've go
But I know why you've come b
It's to put me to the te
To you I'm no goril
Til you see me beat my che

Yeah, I'm a big ol' hairy ap
I weigh four hundred poun
I eat a lot of celery…wild, that
And make a lot of funky soun
Some people think I'm real mea
But that's not what I a
Don't let these nostrils fool yo
I'm as gentle as a lam

You've seen me in the movi
But them movies done me wror
I think I'm much more handson
Than Godzilla or King Kor

I'm a big ol' hairy ap
I'm big and hairy and sma
My brain's a lot like you
It's hard to tell the two apa
So while you're standing there real sm
Analyzing what I d
I'm having twice the fu
Looking right straight back at yo
Yeah, I'm a big ol' hairy ap
And I'm lookin' right back at yo

When Harry finished singing, everyone started clapping and cheering. Rex thought it looked pretty silly standing there slapping your hands together, but Harry seemed to like it, so Rex put four of his arms together and clapped, too. Harry grunted loudly and bowed, then ambled away. Timmy waved goodbye to his gorilla friend.

"Is that grunt Harry's special sound?" asked Rex.

"Yes," answered Timmy, "grunting is a gorilla's special sound."

"I like Harry," said Rex. "I'm going to make him my favorite animal, too."

"Everyone needs to make him their favorite animal," stated Timmy. "Apes are endangered and may someday disappear."

"Harry can come live with me," offered Rex. "I won't let him disappear."

Timmy smiled down at his friend. "I don't think Harry would last very long under the ocean. Come on, let's go see the other animals."

Timmy took Rex to see the lions and tigers and all the other big cats. A pride of lions was lazing in the tall grass. Just as Rex and Timmy stopped to watch them, the papa lion let out a mighty roar. Rex jumped back, startled, but Timmy explained that roaring was the lion's special sound. "Apes grunt and lions roar."

Next, they stopped to look at a very odd creature with horns and two big bumps on each side of its face. "That animal sure is goofy looking," said Rex. "I'm glad I don't look like that!"

"Well, it can't help it," replied Timmy. "I'm sure you look goofy to it." Rex looked down at himself trying to see if he looked goofy. Timmy laughed at his friend's reaction. "She's a warthog and her name is Wanda," said Timmy, reading the sign. "It says those warts on her face are probably there to scare away other animals. And when she runs, her tail goes straight up in the air."

"Eww, warts," said Rex, scrunching up his nose. By now Wanda was very self-conscious because Timmy and Rex were staring at her. Everyone always stared at her; she knew what they were thinking.

Wanda's Lament (CD Track 6)

I'm just an ugly warthog, no one really cares
If I'm here, or if I'm there, or if I'm anywhere
All the other creatures point and laugh at me
My four warts are all they ever see

But when I walk I point my tail straight up to the sky
Suddenly I'm beautiful, I feel like I can fly
For I know that beauty goes far deeper than the skin
If I can't have the skin I love, I'll love the skin I'm in

When I was just a wee hog, my mother said to me
Looks don't really matter, that I guarantee
It's what you've got inside you that makes you so worthwhile
And every time I look at you I smile

Chorus

Beauty is a treasure that can't be bought or sold
Beauty never measures whether you are young or old

If you don't think you're pretty and you just want to cry
Here's a little trick of mine I think you ought to try
Close your eyes and say "I'm beautiful" three times in a row
When you look in the mirror it will be so

And when you walk point your tail straight up to the sky
Suddenly you're beautiful, you'll feel like you can fly
For we know that beauty goes far deeper than the skin
If you can't have the skin you love, then love the skin you're in
If you can't have the skin you love, then love the skin you're in

When Wanda finished her song, Rex was crying. Timmy looked at Rex. "Why are you crying?"

"Be-cause-Wanda-is-sooo-beautiful," replied Rex in between sobs. "I think you're beautiful, Wanda," Rex shouted to her as they turned to go. Wanda blinked back her tears. She gave Rex a grateful smile and then trotted briskly away, her tail pointed high in the air.

"I think you made Wanda feel special," said Timmy. "That was a kind thing to do."

As they made their way around the zoo, Rex saw people eating funny long things covered with yellow stuff. The smell was different from anything he knew under the ocean. "Mmm, I'm hungry," said Rex, looking longingly at the strangely shaped food.

"Me too," said Timmy. "Let's get a hot dog." Timmy walked up to the hot dog stand and bought two hot dogs and two lemonades with the money his mother had given him for their lunch. He and Rex took their hot dogs and drinks over to a table and sat down. Rex just sat there staring at his hot dog. He seemed confused. This dog didn't look anything like Mrs. Hobson's pet dachshund. "Hey, why aren't you eating?" asked Timmy as he took a big bite from his hot dog.

"Is this a dog like Schnitzel?" asked Rex.

Timmy laughed out loud. "No, it's not like Schnitzel or any other dog. It's a wiener, or frankfurter, really."

"I'm glad we're not eating Mrs. Hobson's dachshund," Rex said happily. He took a bite. The mustard squirted all over his face. Timmy just shook his head. He handed Rex a napkin, but Rex preferred wiping the mustard with his arms and then licking each one, just like he did last year with the sticky buns. They finished their lemonades and continued on their way.

"Oh, look, what are those?" asked Rex running ahead. He was pointing to some creatures that were moving around high in the air in a large enclosure.

"They're birds," said Timmy. "Birds can fly because they have wings. This is the aviary where they're kept so they can't fly away."

"Wow!" exclaimed Rex. "Flying looks fun! What are those funny pink birds with the long, skinny legs?"

"Those are flamingos," answered Timmy. "The white birds over there are egrets, and these two over here are toucans. Toucans are cool."

The toucans overheard Timmy's comment. They were accustomed to flattery. They fluffed their feathers and batted their eyes at the boys.

We Are The Toucans (CD Track 8)

Ay muchachos, haven't you heard
We are the most beautiful birds
In all of South America, sí
There are no others more pretty than we
We are the toucans, exotic toucans

Look at all our colors and hues
Brilliant yellows, emeralds and blues
Our golden beaks the boys can't resist
Can you imagine when a toucan tries to kiss
Another toucan, I'm sure that you can

You'll find us up in the trees
From Costa Rica, Brazil and Belize
We snack on tropical fruit
But every once in awhile a bug will suit us fine

We like to bathe in the rain
Why we do we cannot explain
Our tails fold up when we go to sleep
While under our wings our heads we do keep
Because we're toucans, because we can

We'd like to share one little thing
Ay, caramba, we cannot sing
Though we'd like to, birds are supposed to, of course
But each time we try we always sound hoarse
Just like a toucan, sing we no can
Still we're toucans, exotic toucans
I can, you can, we can, who can
Toucan do it better than one, olé!

ola and Chula finished their song and flew to the other side of the aviary.

"I want to fly, too," announced Rex.

"Well, you can't," answered Timmy.

"I want to try," clamored Rex, as he ran to the large oak tree that grew just outside the aviary. Before Timmy could catch him, Rex had climbed to the highest branch.

"Rex, come down," ordered Timmy. "You can't fly; you don't have wings."

"I have *eight* wings!" shouted Rex. "Look!" Rex lifted up his eight arms and jumped out of the tree. But instead of flying like a bird, Rex found himself falling through the air.

He desperately flapped his arms trying to stay up, but he came crashing to the ground with an awful thud. Timmy and several other people ran over to Rex to see if he was all right. His number three arm was bent almost in half.

"Oh, no!" said Timmy. "I think your arm is broken. We better get you to the infirmary. Let's hurry."

Rex was near tears. "My mother is really going to be angry with me. I won't ever be able to come on land again."

By the time they got to the infirmary, Rex's arm was quite swollen; it was hanging at a funny angle. The receptionist took one look at Rex and buzzed Dr. Bugg.

"Dr. Bugg, you have an octopus in the office with a broken arm."

"I'll be right out," shouted Dr. Bugg from behind the wall.

Dr. Bugg was very nearsighted and wore thick round glasses. As he started to come through the door, he walked right smack into the doorframe. He turned and walked right into the other side of the doorframe. He found the opening and shuffled over to where Timmy was standing and felt his arms.

"My, my, what have we here, an octopus with only two arms? Did your other six arms break off?" Dr. Bugg laughed at his joke and slapped his knee. Timmy rolled his eyes.

"I'm not an octopus and I didn't break my arm," declared Timmy. "My friend Rex here is the octopus. He's the one with the broken arm."

Dr. Bugg turned to Rex. "Well, if your arm *was* broken, you wouldn't be an octopus. Octopuses don't have *bones* to break...I don't think. Mmmm. Let me see." He shook Rex's arm and let it drop. Rex yelped in pain; his eyes crossed in his head. "Yep, just a sprain. How did this happen?"

"I was trying to fly," groaned Rex.

"Why, I didn't know octopuses could fly," marveled Dr. Bugg.

"I tried to tell him," said Timmy.

Dr. Bugg wrapped Rex's arm in a bandage. "Try not to move your arm too much, and keep the bandage out of the water for a few days."

"But that's impossible, Dr. Bugg," said Timmy. "Rex is an octopus; he lives under the water."

"You're absolutely right," replied Dr. Bugg. "I wasn't thinking. Just do the best you can, Rex, and your arm should be fine."

"Thanks, Dr. Bugg" said Rex.

Dr. Bugg shuffled slowly back to his office, bumping into the doorframe once again.

"Are you ok?" asked Timmy when they were outside the infirmary. "Does it hurt?"

"Yeah, a little," admitted Rex. "I guess I should have listened to you; I can't fly after all."

"Well, you're lucky you have seven other arms to walk on," said Timmy shaking his head. "Just don't try to be what you're not, OK?"

"OK," answered Rex, "but I really want to fly."

"Hey, there're the elephants," said Timmy excitedly. "Elephants are the largest animals that live on land."

"Look at their funny arms!" giggled Rex.

"Those aren't arms," replied Timmy; "they're trunks. Elephants use their trunks to breathe, to pick up their food, and as a hose to spray water all over themselves."

Rex saw visitors feeding peanuts to a mama and baby elephant.

"Can I feed the elephants, too?" begged Rex. Timmy bought a bag of peanuts and placed a few on the end of Rex's number one arm. Rex held the peanuts out to the baby elephant who gladly picked them up with her small trunk. Then Rex offered some to the mama elephant, Pansy. Pansy swung her trunk over as if she were going to take the peanuts, but instead of taking the peanuts, she curled her trunk around Rex and lifted him over the fence high into the air. She started swinging him around. All the other visitors gasped in horror, but Rex thought this was really fun and squealed with delight. "Hey, Timmy, look at me!"

Look At Me (CD Track 10)

Look at me I'm flying
I'm flying through the air
I've never felt this feeling
Cuz I have to swim everywhere

Look at me I'm soaring
I'm soaring free as a bird
If somebody told you I'm flying
You'd answer them, "that is absurd"

I usually hide inside a shell
Beneath the deep blue sea
But today I'm a flying octopus
Wish everyone could see me

Look at me I'm floating
I feel like a butterfly
I swear if I keep floating
Soon I will reach the sky

Look at me I'm twirling
I'm whirling high off the ground
I'm having the time of my life
On my very own merry-go-round

Look at me I'm flying
I never want to come down
Cuz I'm having the time of my life
On my very own merry-go-round
Yes, I'm having the time of my life
On my very own merry-go-round

Pansy let Rex down and walked back to her baby. Rex ran over to Timmy. "I can fly after all!" He was beaming.

Timmy shook his head and laughed. "Your arms sure get you in trouble. We better get out of here before you "break" another one." Rex wasn't listening; he was still high in the air "flying." Each time he came on land he had more and more fun. He didn't want this day to ever end.

Pansy raised her trunk and trumpeted loudly as if to say goodbye to Rex. Rex tried to imitate the elephant's funny noise. He moved his number one arm up and down pretending it was a trunk.

"Trumpeting is the elephant's special sound," explained Timmy. "It's supposed to sound like a trumpet."

"Wow, I know lots of special sounds," declared Rex happily, "but I still don't know what my special sound is. Do you think we'll find it? I want all my octopus friends to know that I found our special sound."

"Maybe we'll find it when we visit the aquarium," replied Timmy patiently. "That's where they keep the octopuses and other creatures that live in the sea."

"Will they put me in the a-quar-i-um?" Rex asked a bit fearfully.

"I don't think so," laughed Timmy. "I'm sure they have all the octopuses they need."

They walked over to the area where the zebras were grazing. Rex stopped and leaned over the rail trying to get a closer look at the striped animals. He stared at them for quite awhile, concentrating very hard. He tilted his head up and down and from side to side. He even looked at them from upside down.

"What are you doing?" asked Timmy.

"Trying to decide," answered Rex matter of factly.

"Decide what?" Timmy couldn't imagine what Rex was talking about.

"Decide if zebras are white with black stripes or black with white stripes. What do you think?"

Timmy laughed. "Gee, I never thought about it. Let's ask someone. "Excuse me, sir," he said to a man standing nearby. "Are zebras white with black stripes or black with white stripes?"

"Oh, they're black with white stripes," answered the man.

But his wife spoke up and said, "No, Henry, they're white with black stripes!"

"I think you're wrong, Helen," insisted the husband. "I'm positive they're black with white stripes."

"I disagree, Henry," argued his wife.

"Come on, Rex, let's get out of here," said Timmy. "Nobody seems to know for sure."

R ex followed Timmy, all the while looking back at the zebras, trying to decide what they were. The man and woman were still arguing.

Straight ahead of them was a sign in big red letters:

DANGEROUS REPTILES: KEEP OFF THE WALL!

Rex couldn't read the sign, but he was curious to see what was behind it. Using his seven good arms, Rex scampered up the wall before Timmy could stop him. He leaned over to get a closer look and almost lost his balance. Timmy grabbed Rex and pulled him back. "Those are crocodiles and they're dangerous. You *don't* want to fall in there!"

Two crocodiles were submerged in the large pond. Only their bulging eyes were visible above the water. A third crocodile was sunning himself near the wall. He seemed to be grinning. "Look at all those teeth!" exclaimed Rex.

The crocodile opened one eye and saw Timmy and Rex staring at him. "That's Chompers," Timmy told Rex. "He's the oldest and meanest crocodile in the zoo."

C hompers didn't like that Timmy and Rex were staring at him, so he decided to frighten them a little. After all, he was a crocodile, and that's what crocodiles did best.

CHOMPERS' SONG (CD Track 12)

Why're you starin' at me boys, have you never seen a crocodile
 I bet you think I'm real friendly, but don't be fooled by my crocosmile

And don't confuse me with an alligator, a gator's tame compared to me
 I'm giving you fair warning boys, I'm the mean one of the family

My skin is hard and scaly, my disposition's a little bit harsh
 I'm cranky all the time because I always get up on the wrong side of the marsh

If you're thinkin' that you might want to wrestle me, I hope you're thinkin' you just might lose
 Cuz I'm gonna put up one heck of a fight before I wind up as a pair of shoes

You'll find me in the land down under, in Africa and Asia too
 You'll find me in the Florida Everglades, just lying in wait for you

And if you ever take a trip to Egypt to see the pyramids along the Nile
 Be careful you don't fall out of the boat, or you'll be dinner for some crocodile

So stop your starin' at me boys, I think it's time you were on your way
 I'd like to have you for lunch sometime, if you ever come back some day
 I'd like to have you for lunch sometime, if you ever come back some day

"Ooooh," shuddered Rex. "I sure hope I'm not lunch for any crocodile."

"You almost were," teased Timmy.

"I bet Chompers is too mean to have a special sound," said Rex.

Chompers chuckled to himself. "I'll show 'em *special*." He opened his jagged, toothy jaws as wide as he could and snapped them shut with a ferocious, frightening *crunch!* Then he slipped into the water to join his friends.

Rex was shaking a little. Timmy chuckled. "I guess we know what Chompers' special sound is. Come on, I think it's time we went to the aquarium to see if we can find your sound!" Rex was so excited he ran and skipped all the way to the aquarium. He couldn't wait to see the octopuses.

Inside the aquarium were several large tanks full of fish and underwater sea creatures. Now it was Rex's turn to play teacher. He explained to Timmy about the many

sea creatures swimming in the giant tank.

"Oh, there are the jelly fish; they can sting you. Uh oh, look over there at that moray eel. I better not let him see me," said Rex hiding behind Timmy. "Octopuses are moray eels' favorite things to eat."

"He can't get to you from in there," Timmy assured Rex, but Rex didn't want to take any chances and stayed close behind Timmy.

At the last tank, Rex began jumping up and down and shouting, "Here are the octopuses!" He started waving at them and then realized that he recognized one of them. "Oh, I think I see my friend, Inky! Hi Inky, hi Inky," shouted Rex as he tapped on the glass trying to get Inky's attention.

When Inky saw Rex, he swam up to the glass and waved his eight arms at his friend. Inky pointed to Rex's bandaged arm with a questioning look on his face. Rex tried to tell Inky what happened, but Inky couldn't understand anything Rex was saying through the glass.

Rex pouted. "I wish Inky and I could hear each other. I bet we could if we had a special sound like a bark, or a roar, or a trumpet."

"It looks to me as if you and Inky are communicating OK *without* having a special sound," observed Timmy.

"Yeah, but I really want to have my own sound. All the other animals have one. What will I tell my friends?"

"Gosh, Rex, it's possible that octopuses don't have a special sound, but you don't need a special sound to be special. It's just one part of who we are." Timmy was trying to comfort his friend. "All creatures have something special, whether it's a roar, or warts, or a large yellow beak. Octopuses have arms that can grow back. You have a well-developed brain, and you can change colors, too. That's pretty neat."

Rex thought about what Timmy had said and it cheered him up. "Yeah, I guess you're right. We should all be happy with what we have." He smiled at Inky and waved goodbye. Inky waved back and swam away.

"It's late," said Timmy. "You better get back to the water."

"I know," sighed Rex, not wanting to leave. Rex and Timmy walked back to the blue umbrella where they had met that morning.

"Thanks," said Rex. "I'll see you next summer."

"And I'll be waiting for you right here," declared Timmy. "And don't break any more arms!" They both laughed and high-fived each other just as they did last summer, and this summer, and just as they would do next year..

Gimme Five (Reprise) (CD Track 14)

(Timmy):
Gimme five, my friend, when you're back again
I'll be waiting here
Beneath this blue umbrella
Exact same time next year
We'll slide down that sand dune
Then climb back up again
That's what we'll do next summer
Gimme five again

(Rex):
Gimme five, my friend, when I'm back again
Right here's where I'll be
Beneath this blue umbrella
You can count on me
I'll be Silver Surfer
You be Superman
That's what we'll do next summer
Gimme five again

(Both):
This time we were careful
This time we were smart
(Rex):You did not let me dry up and die
(Timmy):I promised 'n' crossed my heart

(Both)
Gimme five, my friend, around the bend
We'll find the carousel
We'll ride the magic horses
And munch on caramel
We'll float down the river
Like Tom Sawyer and Huck Finn
That's what we'll do next summer
Gimme five again
That's what we'll do next summer
Gimme five again
(Whistle)
Gimme five again
Not one, two, three, four
But gimme five again, yeah!